Malcolm Carrick

THE VIKING PRESS   NEW YORK

First American Edition

Copyright © 1975 by Malcolm Carrick
All rights reserved
Published in 1976 by The Viking Press, Inc.
625 Madison Avenue, New York, N.Y. 10022
Printed in U.S.A.

1   2   3   4   5   80   79   78   77   76

Library of Congress Cataloging in Publication Data
Carrick, Malcolm.   Splodges.
1. Painting—Technique—Juvenile literature.
2. Painting—Themes, motives—Juvenile literature.
I. Title.   ND1146.C37   1976   751.4′02′4054   75–42396
ISBN 0–670–66451–0

One day I sat down to paint
a picture-book when . . .
drip drip.
"Oh bother!" I said.

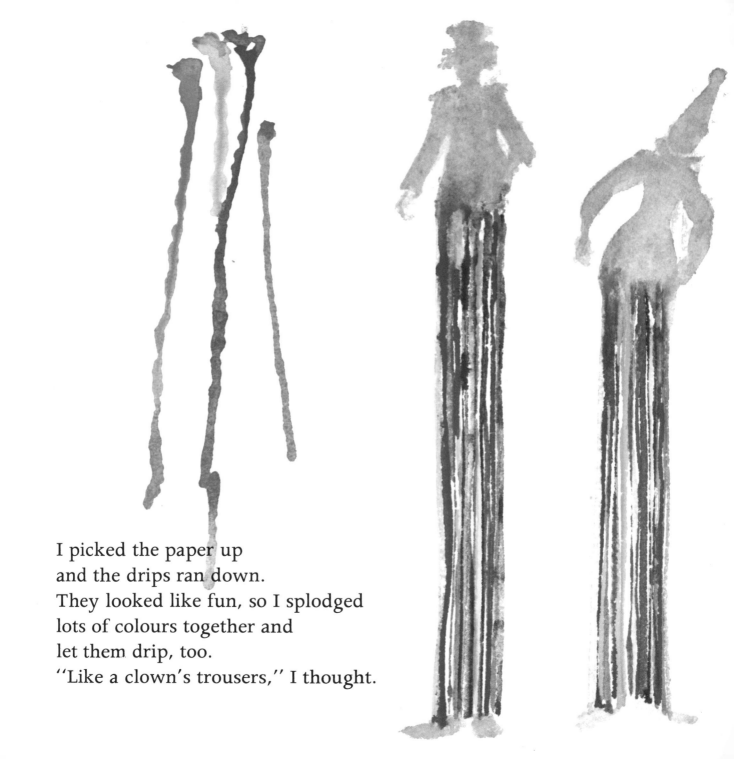

I picked the paper up
and the drips ran down.
They looked like fun, so I splodged
lots of colours together and
let them drip, too.
"Like a clown's trousers," I thought.

One drip went sideways and I tried
to catch it with a big brush –
SPLODGE, SPLODGE, SPLODGE –
but I missed.
''Some trees look like that,''
I said to myself.

I decided to start again, but I spilt
water all over my clean sheet of paper.
When I tried to paint on it the paint splodged
into flowery shapes. Some of them looked a bit like fish,
so that's what I made them into.

Some of the other shapes
looked like kites,
so I added strings
and children to fly them.

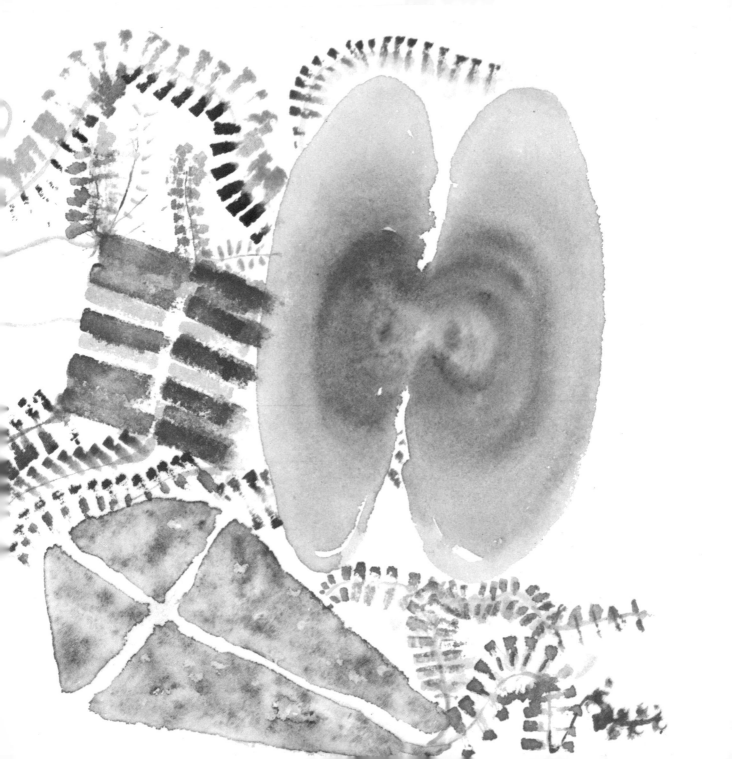

Well, then I lost my brushes,
and knocked over more paint
looking for them.
I tried to blow the paint away,
but it went into lines and bobbles.
I tried blowing with a straw.

These look like trees . . .
or knobbly knees.
Add a body, for a laugh,
and spots to make a tall giraffe.

Dancers, too, with arms and legs
bending in the air,
leap and jump to catch the breeze
that ruffles through their hair.

Then I drew with a candle,
thinking it was a crayon.
The paper looked empty,
but when I painted over it,
the drawing came through,
like magic.

"I must get on with this book,"
I sighed, and then found
someone had left building bricks
in my paint. Cheek!
I pressed them onto the paper
to clean them.

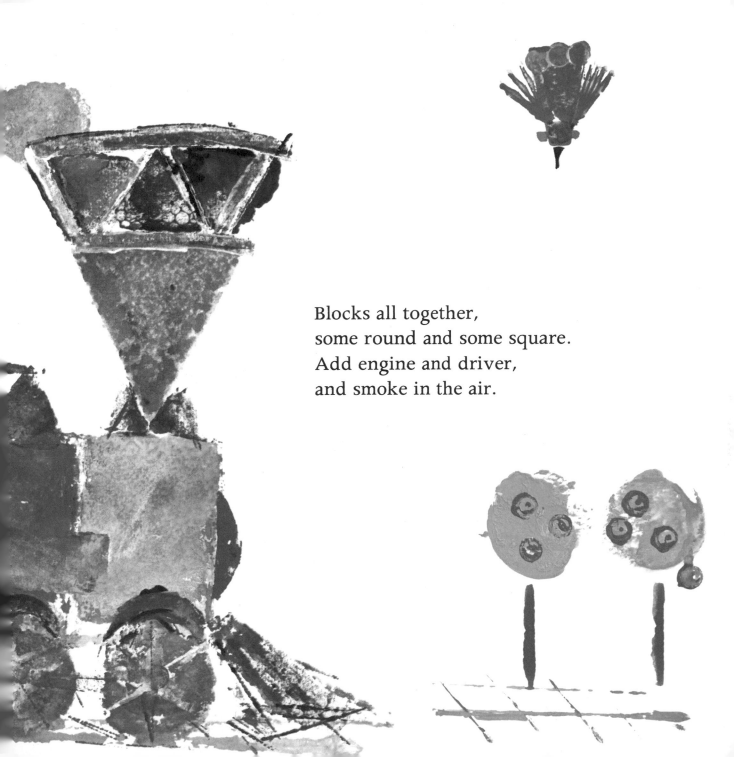

Blocks all together,
some round and some square.
Add engine and driver,
and smoke in the air.

Now the blocks were covered in thick paint
so I scraped them along the paper to clean them.
With lots of thick colours on the paper
I scraped a rainbow, and found I could wobble
the brick to get a snakey shape.

Even my ruler was covered in paint.
I pressed it on the paper to clean it,
and it left a thin straight line.
''Could be a ship's mast,'' I thought,
and I carried on, dipping the edge
of the ruler in other colours
and pressing it onto the paper.

Then I found my two crayons were
tied together with an elastic band.
"I'll never start this book," I said,
as I pushed them over the page.
When I found my brushes
I held them together in the same way –
and see what happened!

Then a leaf blew in from my window
and landed with a SHHPLOP,
right in my paint.

I pressed the leaf hard onto some paper,
and soon discovered that leaves
could make pictures, too.

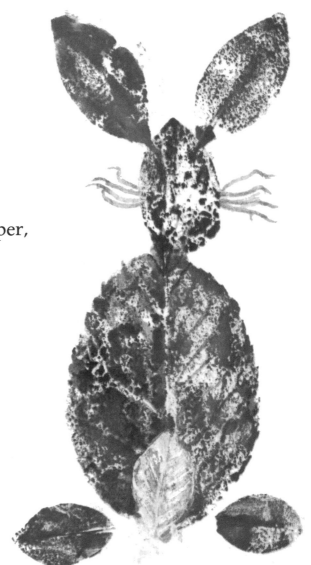

By this time my hands were covered in thick paint and I had left finger marks everywhere. They soon became a rooster's crest . . .
or a peacock's feathers.

Or a dragon's body,
hard and scaly –
fire for his mouth,
and a point for his taily.

Finally I mixed up some runny paint and was
just about to start this book, when the
paint ran down the middle of my paper.
''I give up!'' I said as I folded the paper in half

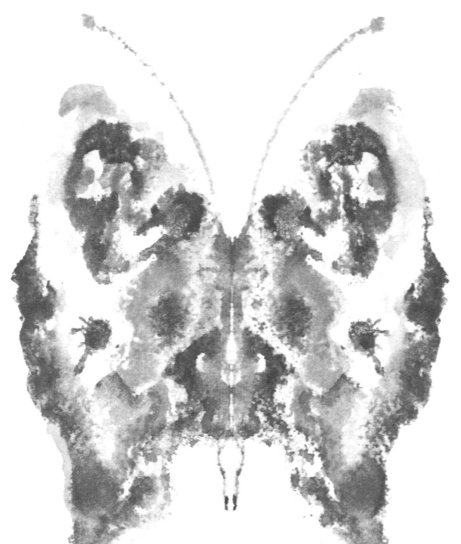

and pressed it down hard. But instead of throwing it
away, I opened it up and there was a butterfly!
My drips and smudges certainly have turned into
the most amazing things.

What about yours?